Colusa County Free Library

P9-AGI-940

THE ADVENTURES OF
SIMPLE SIMON

RETOLD AND WITH PICTURES BY
CHRIS CONOVER

A SUNBURST BOOK

FARRAR STRAUS GIROUX

COLUSA COUNTY LIBRARY

Copyright © 1987 by Chris Conover
All rights reserved
Library of Congress catalog card number: 87-45755
Published in Canada by Collins Publishers, Toronto
Printed in the United States of America
Designed by Cynthia Krupat
First edition, 1987
Sunburst edition, 1989

For Barry, with love,
and with fond thanks to
Stephen Roxburgh and
Cynthia Krupat

Simple Simon met a pieman,
Going to the fair.
Said Simple Simon to the pieman,
"Let me taste your ware."

Said the pieman to Simple Simon,
"First give me a penny."
Said Simple Simon to the pieman,

"Indeed, I have not any."

He went to see if purple plums
Grew upon a thistle.
This pricked his fingers very much,
Which made poor Simon whistle.

He tried to take a bird's nest,
Built upon a bough.
It broke in two, and Simon fell
Upon a spotted cow.

Simon rode the spotted cow,
Up the streets and down,
Searching for a cottontail
All around the town.

Simon went a-fishing,
To catch a blubber whale.
All the water he had got
Was in a wooden pail.

He went to slide upon the ice,
Before the ice would bear.
He fell in and banged his shin,
But Simon didn't care.

Simon tried to catch a bird
And thought he couldn't fail,
Because he had a bit of salt
To put upon his tail.

He tried his best to bag the bird,
But it flew away.
He said,

"I cannot catch him,
Because he will not stay."

Simon made a snowball
And put it in a pot.
He set it down beside the fire
And served it piping hot.

He washed himself with polish
And gave his face a shine.
Then he buffed his shoes with soap
And hung them on the line.

He took some water in a sieve,
But soon it all slipped through.
And now poor Simple Simon
Bids you all "*Adieu!*"

Simon says, "Can you find these rhymes in the pictures?"

Little Jack Horner
Three Little Kittens
Humpty Dumpty
Little Miss Muffet
This Little Pig
Pease Porridge Hot
Twinkle, Twinkle, Little Star
Sing a Song of Sixpence
Wee Willie Winkie
Rub-a-Dub-Dub
Three Blind Mice
The Queen of Hearts
Peter, Peter, Pumpkin Eater
Jack Be Nimble
Hey Diddle Diddle
Jack and Jill